WATER POWER

Christine Webster

AV² by Weigl brings you media enhanced books that support active learning.

AV² provides enriched content that supplements and complements this book. Weigl's AV² books strive to create inspired learning and engage young minds for a total learning experience.

Go to **www.av2books.com**, and enter this book's unique code. You will have access to video, audio, web links, quizzes, a slide show, and activities.

BOOK CODE

Q 8 8 7 7 1 3

Audio
Listen to sections of the book read aloud.

Video
Watch informative video clips.

Web Link
Find research sites and play interactive games.

Try This!
Complete activities and hands-on experiments.

Due to the dynamic nature of the Internet, some of the URLs and activities provided as part of AV² by Weigl may have changed or ceased to exist. AV² by Weigl accepts no responsibility for any such changes. All media enhanced books are regularly monitored to update addresses and sites in a timely manner. Contact AV² by Weigl at 1-866-649-3445 or av2books@weigl.com with any questions, comments, or feedback.

Published by AV² by Weigl
350 5th Avenue, 59th Floor
New York, NY 10118
Website: www.av2books.com   www.weigl.com

Library of Congress Cataloging-in-Publication Data

Webster, Christine.
 Water power / Christine Webster.
    p. cm. -- (Water science. Water Power)
 Includes index.
 ISBN 978-1-61690-005-2 (hardcover : alk. paper) -- ISBN 978-1-61690-011-3 (softcover : alk. paper) -- ISBN 978-1-61690-017-5 (e-book)
 1. Hydroelectric power plants--Juvenile literature. 2. Water-power--Juvenile literature. I. Title.
 TC146.W43 2011
 621.2'0422--dc22
                          2009050984

Printed in the United States of America in North Mankato, Minnesota
1 2 3 4 5 6 7 8 9 0 14 13 12 11 10

052010
WEP264000

Project Coordinator Heather C. Hudak
Design Terry Paulhus

Photo Credits
Every reasonable effort has been made to trace ownership and to obtain permission to reprint copyright material. The publishers would be pleased to have any errors or omissions brought to their attention so that they may be corrected in subsequent printings.

Weigl acknowledges Getty Images as its primary image supplier for this title.

CONTENTS

Often, electricity is made by burning coal or running a nuclear power plant. These energy sources are not environmentally friendly. Only some types of electricity come from green sources, such as **hydroelectric dams**. Turning off the lights when leaving a room and unplugging appliances when they are not in use are two ways to save energy and help make the world a greener place.

Studying Water Power

Electricity makes machines run. Coal, gas, and oil are often used to create electricity. These sources are called fossil fuels, and they will run out over time. There is a limited supply of fossil fuels because they are found only in some parts of the world. Fossil fuels can harm the environment.

Water can be used to create electricity. Water power is a **renewable** source of energy because the flow of water is part of the water cycle. Water **recycles** itself through the water cycle. Electricity converted from water power is called hydroelectricity.

People have used water's energy for thousands of years. Ancient Greeks and Romans used **waterwheels** to grind corn and wheat. Ocean currents have brought many explorers to their destinations. River currents have pulled heavy logs to sawmills. Water power is still used to saw wood and power mills and factories.

■ About 10 percent of the United States' electric power comes from hydroelectricity.

Water for Electricity

Water is constantly moving. Tides and currents help move water around the world. Currents are the movements of bodies of water in a certain direction. Tides are the regular rise and fall of water levels in the ocean. In most places, the tide rises and falls twice each day. The movement of water is powerful and creates energy. Special machines change this energy into electricity.

MODERN HYDROPOWER PLANT

Electricity is created from water power at hydropower plants. This diagram shows the process of turning water into electricity.

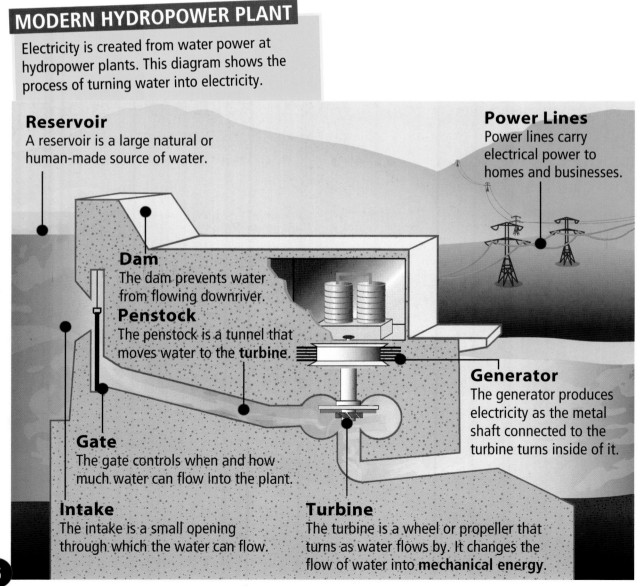

Reservoir
A reservoir is a large natural or human-made source of water.

Power Lines
Power lines carry electrical power to homes and businesses.

Dam
The dam prevents water from flowing downriver.

Penstock
The penstock is a tunnel that moves water to the **turbine**.

Generator
The generator produces electricity as the metal shaft connected to the turbine turns inside of it.

Gate
The gate controls when and how much water can flow into the plant.

Intake
The intake is a small opening through which the water can flow.

Turbine
The turbine is a wheel or propeller that turns as water flows by. It changes the flow of water into **mechanical energy**.

The energy created by water falling from a high level to a low level can be used to create electricity. Large waterfalls, such as Niagara Falls, create electricity in this way. Falling water is directed into long pipes connected to a power station. The force of the moving water makes waterwheels spin inside the power station. The spinning waterwheels cause machines called turbines to turn. These turbines create electricity.

HOW TURBINES WORK

This image shows the parts of a turbine and how they work together to create electricity.

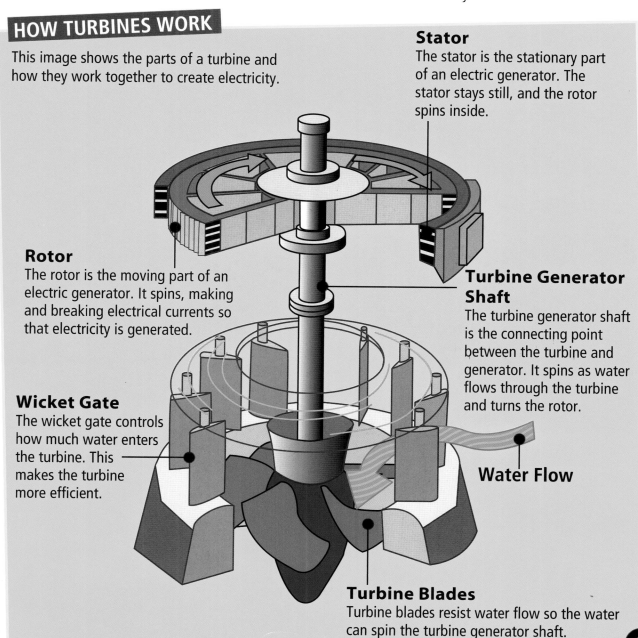

Stator
The stator is the stationary part of an electric generator. The stator stays still, and the rotor spins inside.

Rotor
The rotor is the moving part of an electric generator. It spins, making and breaking electrical currents so that electricity is generated.

Turbine Generator Shaft
The turbine generator shaft is the connecting point between the turbine and generator. It spins as water flows through the turbine and turns the rotor.

Wicket Gate
The wicket gate controls how much water enters the turbine. This makes the turbine more efficient.

Water Flow

Turbine Blades
Turbine blades resist water flow so the water can spin the turbine generator shaft.

Reasons to Use Water Power

On this page, you will learn that water power has advantages and disadvantages. Can you list some other advantages or disadvantages of using water power?

ADVANTAGES

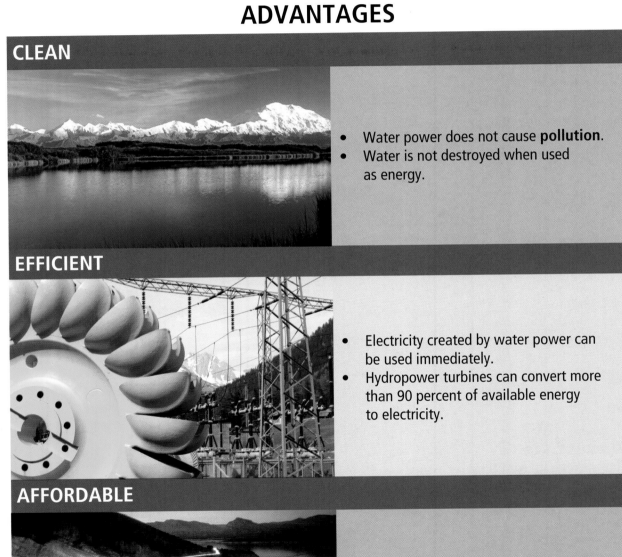

CLEN

- Water power does not cause **pollution**.
- Water is not destroyed when used as energy.

EFFICIENT

- Electricity created by water power can be used immediately.
- Hydropower turbines can convert more than 90 percent of available energy to electricity.

AFFORDABLE

- Hydropower is less expensive to create than power from fossil fuels.
- Hydroelectric dams have a long life.

Do you think using water to create electricity is a good idea or a bad idea? Explain your answer.

DISADVANTAGES

EXPENSIVE UPFRONT COSTS

- Dams are expensive to build.
- Dams must be built to meet very high standards.

ENVIRONMENTAL CHANGE

- Building dams destroys the environment and can cause flooding.
- Hydropower plants heat up water. Heating up water changes the environment and can cause harm to plants and animals that live there.

AFFECTS WILDLIFE

- Turbines can hurt animals in the water.
- The location of dams can hurt fish **spawning**.

The Waterwheel and Steam Power

The waterwheel was the first machine created to use water power. Waterwheels need moving water, so they are built on rivers and streams. Flowing water strikes the wheel's blades in the water. The water pushes the blades, causing the wheel to turn. The spinning waterwheel powers machines. Power from a waterwheel is not always reliable. During winter, water often freezes. Sometimes, a **drought** leaves people with no power.

Over time, people found that steam could be used as a source of power. Water boiled under pressure makes steam that is full of energy. Inventors created steam engines to use this energy. A steam engine needs a **boiler**. The boiler boils water to produce steam under pressure. This creates energy. The steam in the boiler expands and pushes against a piston or turbine.

■ At one time, trains used steam engines. However, only 35 percent of the energy used to heat the water to produce steam becomes electricity.

Water Power Through History

2,000 Years Ago | 1880 | 1885 | 1890 | 1900 | 1910 | 1920 | 1930 | 1940 | 1950 | 1960 | 1970 | 1980 | 1990 | 2000 | 2010

1 — **2 3 4** — **5 6 7** — **8** — **9 10** — **11**

1 More than 2,000 years ago
Hydropower is used by the Greeks to turn waterwheels for grinding wheat into flour.

2 1880
Michigan's Grand Rapids Electric Light and Power Company begins generating electricity. It produces enough power to light 16 lamps.

3 1881
Niagara Falls city street lamps begin running on hydropower.

4 1882
The world's first hydroelectric power plant begins operation on the Fox River in Appleton, Wisconsin.

5 1886
About 45 water-powered electric plants are active in the United States and Canada.

6 1887
San Bernardino, California, opens the first hydroelectric plant in the West.

7 1889
Two hundred electric plants in the United States use water power for some or all power production.

8 1920
Hydropower provides 25 percent of U.S. electricity. Laws are created to decide who will be allowed to build hydropower stations on public land.

9 1937
Bonneville Dam begins operation on the Columbia River. It is the first dam built by the U.S. government.

10 1940
Hydropower provides 40 percent of electricity in the United States.

11 2003
Only about 10 percent of U.S. electricity comes from hydropower.

Water Power Around the World

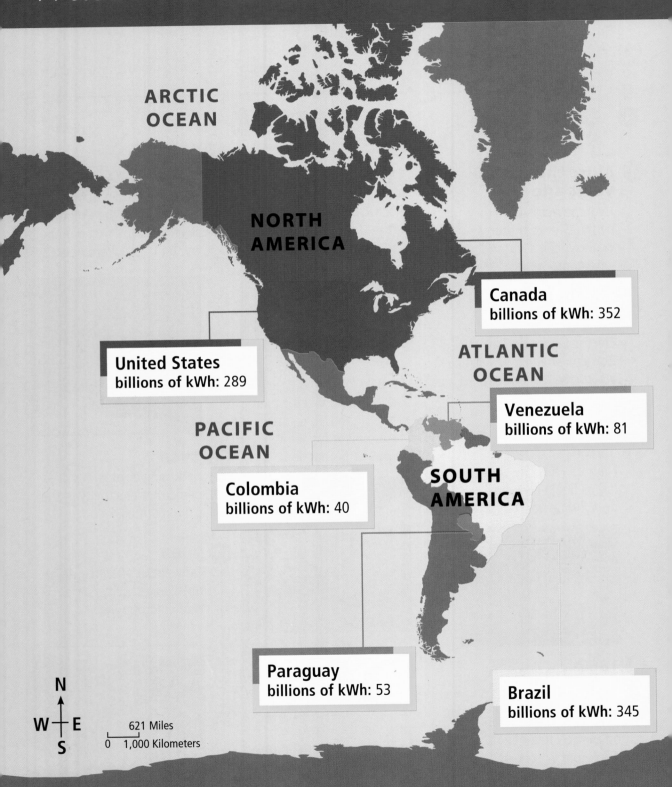

ARCTIC
OCEAN

NORTH
AMERICA

Canada
billions of kWh: 352

ATLANTIC
OCEAN

United States
billions of kWh: 289

Venezuela
billions of kWh: 81

PACIFIC
OCEAN

SOUTH
AMERICA

Colombia
billions of kWh: 40

Paraguay
billions of kWh: 53

Brazil
billions of kWh: 345

N
W E
S

621 Miles
0   1,000 Kilometers

WHAT HAVE YOU LEARNED ABOUT WATER POWER?

This map shows the top water power producing countries around the world by kilowatts per hour (kWh). A watt is a unit of measurement used to measure electricity. Use this map, and research online to answer these questions.

1. Which country makes the most water power?
2. Why are some countries listed on the map able to produce more water power than other countries?

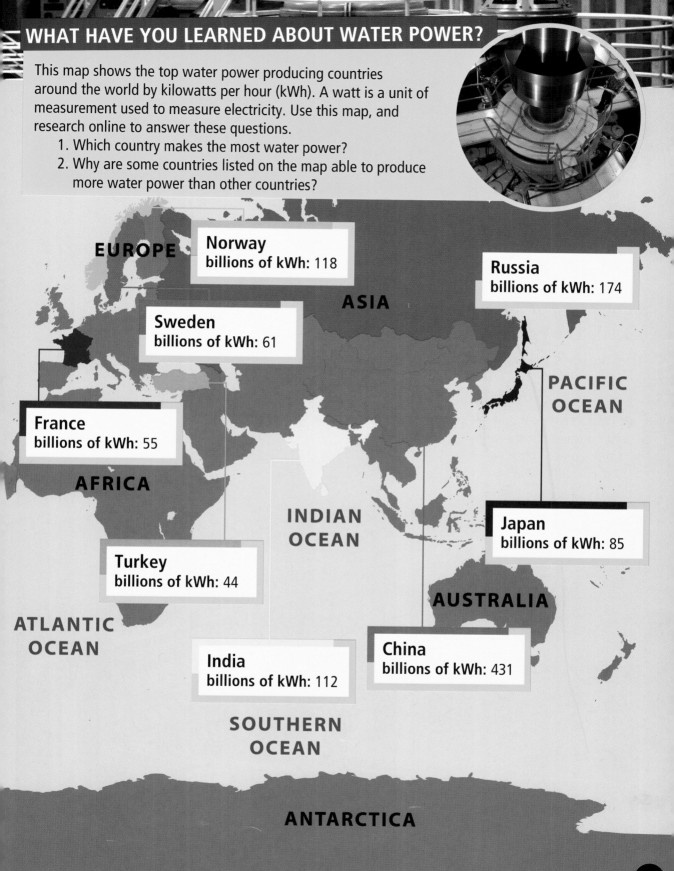

EUROPE

Norway
billions of kWh: 118

Russia
billions of kWh: 174

ASIA

Sweden
billions of kWh: 61

PACIFIC
OCEAN

France
billions of kWh: 55

AFRICA

INDIAN
OCEAN

Japan
billions of kWh: 85

Turkey
billions of kWh: 44

AUSTRALIA

ATLANTIC
OCEAN

China
billions of kWh: 431

India
billions of kWh: 112

SOUTHERN
OCEAN

ANTARCTICA

Hydroelectric Dams and Stored Power

Dams are built to stop flooding, to provide water, and to create electricity. Dams are made of concrete that is **reinforced** with steel. Most dams have a curved shape. This provides a much stronger structure against water currents.

As water collects behind a dam, the energy level in the water builds. When the water is released, the flowing water gains speed. The flowing water passes through turbines that change the water's energy into electricity.

■ Hydropower can only be used in some parts of the world because power plants need fast-flowing water throughout the year.

Reservoirs store water for creating electricity. They are found behind dams. A reservoir is like an **artificial** lake. The deeper the water in the reservoir, the more power can be produced. Water can be directed back into the reservoir to be reused.

Reservoirs also supply drinking water. People can fish in reservoirs. Reservoirs can even be used for water sports such as kayaking.

■ Large dams make up 19 percent of the world's supply of electricity. For many countries around the world, hydropower accounts for more than half of their electricity supply.

Water is a limited resource. Fresh water is used faster than nature can **replenish** its supply. In the future, this could lead to water shortages, and people will not be able to get all of the water they need to live. Some ways to help save water include fixing leaky faucets and turning off the water while brushing teeth. If everyone on Earth makes an effort to save water, there will be more water for future use.

Tidal Power

The energy in tides can be used to create electricity. Tidal power is turned into electricity using a huge dam built across a river **estuary**. The tidal waters flow through tunnels in the dam. The water then passes through turbines to produce electricity.

Tidal power stations can only create power when the tide is flowing in or out. This happens for about 10 hours per day. Only about 20 sites in the world can be used to create energy from tides. The Rance Tidal Power Station in France is one such facility. It is the largest tidal power station in the world.

TIDAL POWER

A tidal power plant works much like a regular hydropower plant, except water flows two ways. The turbine creates spin when water flows in and when it flows out. Tidal water builds up in estuaries. When water is released from the estuary, the turbines move, creating electricity.

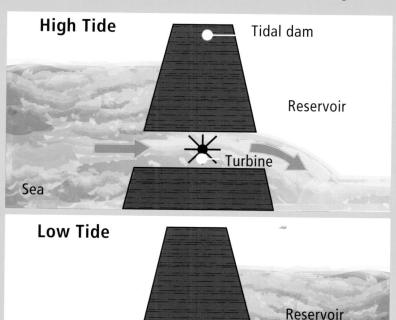

High Tide

Tidal dam

Reservoir

Turbine

Sea

Water flows into the reservoir from the sea at high tide. The dam only allows the water to pass through a small opening. Inside sits the turbine. The water turns the turbine to produce electricity.

Low Tide

Reservoir

Sea

Stored water flows from the reservoir to the sea during low tide. The stored water turns the turbines to produce electricity.

Environmental Issues

Water power is clean. It does not release harmful gases into the air. Still, using dams to create electricity affects the environment.

When a dam is built, the land around the dam is usually destroyed. To save the environment, plants and trees need to be replanted. Rocks need to be replaced. Construction of dams can also cause flooding. The environment may never return to normal.

■ People often are affected by dam construction. As many as 80 million people in the world have been sent away from their homes to make room for a dam.

What is a Hydroelectric Engineer?

Pelton Wheel

Hydroelectric engineers build and maintain hydropower plants. They also oversee the output of the plant.

Lester Allan Pelton

Lester Allan Pelton lived in California in 1849. Gold had been discovered in California, and many people moved there. Pelton worked as a carpenter and **millwright**. The gold mining industry was growing fast, so there was great demand for new ways to power machinery and mills. Waterwheels did not work well in mountain creeks.

While watching a waterwheel, Pelton noticed that the wheel spun faster when water hit the edge of the wheel than when it hit the center. Lester Pelton created a new, more efficient design for a water turbine. His design is called the Pelton wheel.

Working Conditions
Hydroelectric engineers work in and around hydropower plants.

Tools
Hydroelectric engineers do many calculations. Computers, calculators, and measuring tools help them do this. Engineers make blueprints to communicate to others how to build their designs.

Blueprints

Eight Facts About Water Power

The state of Washington creates more hydroelectric power than any other U.S. state. About 87 percent of Washington's electricity is produced by hydroelectric facilities.

Water power is the most efficient and least expensive method of creating electricity in the United States.

Hydropower can be used any place in the world that has falling water.

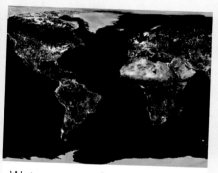

Water creates about 20 percent of the world's electricity.

Canada is the world's largest producer of hydroelectricity.

Hydropower is mainly used to produce electricity.

The United States is the world's second largest producer of hydroelectricity.

Most hydropower in the United States is used in the northwestern states. It accounts for 70 percent of the electricity produced in the northwest.

Water Power Brain Teasers

1 Name two ways in which water moves.

2 What causes a waterwheel to move?

3 What is another name for water power?

4 What stores water behind a dam?

5 Can Earth run out of water?

6 Which country is the number one producer of water power?

7 What machines create electricity from water energy?

8 Does steam have power?

9 What are dams used for?

10 What is the most efficient way to create electricity in the United States?

ANSWERS: 1. Currents and tides 2. Moving water 3. Hydroelectricity 4. A reservoir 5. No. Water recycles itself through the water cycle. Clean water must still be protected, however. 6. Canada 7. Turbines 8. Yes. Steam powers some engines. 9. Dams are used to provide water, stop flooding, and create electricity. 10. Water power

Build a Waterwheel

You can build your own waterwheel to see the power of water in action.

Tools Needed

a foam ball

a long skewer or stick about twice the length of the ball

water

a sink or large bowl

plastic spoons

a large cup

Directions

1 Poke the skewer through the center of the ball.

2 Wiggle the skewer until the ball easily spins around it.

3 Place the plastic spoons evenly in a row around the ball. Stick the handles into the ball, and make sure the scoops all face up.

4 Hold the ball by the skewer over the sink or bowl.

5 Fill the cup with water. Raise the cup of water as high as you can. Pour the water over your waterwheel. What happens? Try pouring the water from higher and lower heights. Does the height change how the waterwheel spins? Look at the picture of the waterwheel above. How does it compare to your waterwheel?

Words to Know

artificial: something made by people, not nature

boiler: a large tank that heats water and turns it into steam

dams: walls built across streams or rivers to hold back and control water

drought: a long period with no rain

estuary: the mouth of a river where the river meets the sea and is affected by the tides

hydroelectric: electricity made from water power

mechanical energy: the energy of motion used to perform work

millwright: a person who sets up machinery in a mill

pollution: harmful materials such as gases, chemicals, and waste that dirty air, water, and soil

recycles: returns to an original condition so a process can begin again

reinforced: supported with a stronger material

renewable: energy sources that do not run out, such as solar power or wind energy

replenish: return to original level

spawning: when fish lay eggs

turbine: a machine that transfers the water's energy so it can be turned into electricity

waterwheels: machines that convert flowing water into usable energy

Index

Log on to www.av2books.com

AV² by Weigl brings you media enhanced books that support active learning. Go to **www.av2books.com**, and enter the special code inside the front cover of this book. You will gain access to enriched and enhanced content that supplements and complements this book. Content includes video, audio, web links, quizzes, a slide show, and activities.

Audio
Listen to sections of the book read aloud.

Video
Watch informative video clips.

Web Link
Find research sites and play interactive games.

Try This!
Complete activities and hands-on experiments.

WHAT'S ONLINE?

 Try This!
Complete activities and hands-on experiments.

 Web Link
Find research sites and play interactive games.

 Video
Watch informative video clips.

EXTRA FEATURES

Pages 6-7 Try this activity about a hydropower plant

Pages 10-11 Use this timeline activity to test your knowledge of world events

Pages 12-13 See if you can identify water power around the world

Pages 18-19 Write about a day in the life of a hydroelectric engineer

Page 22 Try the activity in the book, then play an interactive game

Pages 8-9 Link to more information about the benefits of water power

Pages 16-17 Find out more about tidal power

Pages 18-19 Learn more about being a hydroelectric engineer

Page 20 Link to facts about water power

Pages 4-5 Watch a video about water power

Pages 8-9 Check out a video about oceans

Pages 14-15 View a hydroelectric dam in action

 Audio
Hear introductory au at the top of every p

Key Words
Study vocabulary, and play a matching word game.

Slide Show
View images and captions, and try a writing activity.

AV² Quiz
Take this quiz to test your knowledge